SHE'S MY DAD!

**A Story for Children Who Have
a Transgender Parent or Relative**

Sarah Savage
Illustrated by Joules Garcia

Jessica Kingsley Publishers
London and Philadelphia

First published in Great Britain in 2020 by Jessica Kingsley Publishers
An Hachette Company

1

A CIP catalogue record for this title is available from the
British Library and the Library of Congress

ISBN 978 1 78592 615 0
eISBN 978 1 78592 616 7

Printed and bound in China by Leo Paper Products

Jessica Kingsley Publishers' policy is to use papers that are natural,
renewable and recyclable products and made from wood grown
in sustainable forests. The logging and manufacturing processes
are expected to conform to the environmental regulations of
the country of origin.

Jessica Kingsley Publishers
73 Collier Street
London N1 9BE, UK

www.jkp.com

Hi! My name is Mini. I am 6 years old and I love kittens more than anything in the world.

Did you know that it takes a whole year
for a kitten to become a cat?

The second thing I love more than anything in the world is my dad. Every day we make breakfast together and get ready to go out.

"Don't forget to brush your teeth, Mini!"

Today we are helping out at the cat rescue centre.

Dad says it's important to help others, so we come here every Saturday morning to help clean up.

I am in charge of
kitten cuddles!

Afterwards, we get ready for Grampa's birthday party.
Dad and I take turns to paint each other's nails.

Oh, didn't I tell you?

My dad is a **she**!

My dad's name is Haley. She used to be a he but now she is a **she**! Last year she did this thing called **transition**.

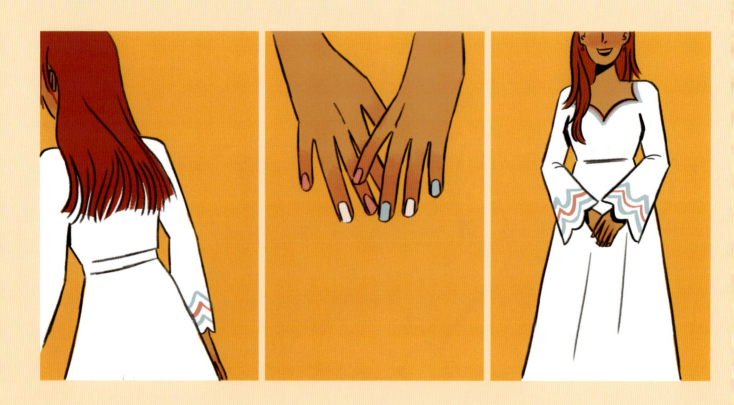

She grew her hair long, painted her nails in bright colours and started wearing different clothes.

When she told me about transition it sounded a bit scary at first, but she said,

"I will always be your dad and I will always love you very much,"

so this made me feel better.

Dad changed her name to Haley and asked me to use the pronouns **she/her** instead of **he/him**.

Sometimes I call her
Dad and sometimes
I call her Haley.

She likes both.

Dad smiles and laughs a lot more now,

so I am happy too.

As part of her transition, Dad went
to the hospital to have surgery.

When we went to visit her I made her a card and
gave her my favourite teddy bear for cuddles.

Though Haley's outsides might have changed,
inside she's still my dad.

Look at our pretty nails!

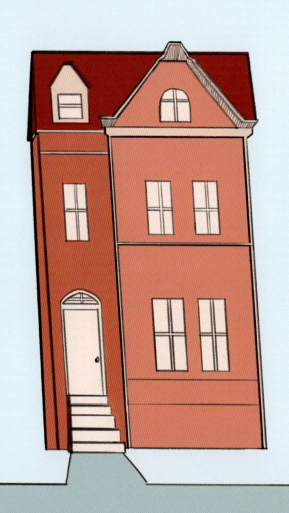

We have to hurry to get to Grampa's house, we're late!

Happy birthday Grampa!

My favourite cousin is here!

I like her because her name is Kat!

Kat's dad is my Uncle Mark. He gives Daddy and me a great big hug and tells me to hurry and wash up for dinner.

I love family dinners.
Everybody is here!

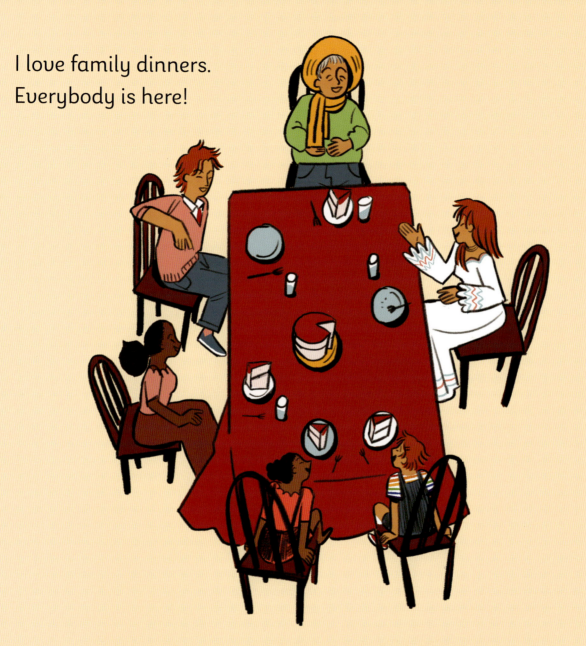

I sit next to Kat because she doesn't like red
birthday cake icing and shares it with me!

Dad is telling everybody a funny story, even Grampa is laughing at her silly jokes. Kat laughs and says to me,

"Mini, I really like Haley, he's so funny."

"No, not he, my dad is a **she**!" I say to Kat.
"It makes her feel sad when people use the wrong pronouns."

It makes me feel sad too because I love my dad very much.

"Oh, I'm sorry," Kat says, "I didn't mean to hurt you or Haley."

"It's OK, I know you didn't mean to," I say.
"I did the same too when Dad started her transition.
It took me a while to get used to it."

But now when anyone asks about Haley,
I loudly and proudly say,

"She's my dad!"

READING GUIDE

What pronouns does Hayley's dad use?

Why was Mini upset with their cousin Kat?

Why is it important to use the right pronouns when speaking about someone?

What should you do if you refer to someone by the wrong pronouns?

If you do not know what pronouns someone uses, why is it important to ask?

When someone asks Mini about Haley, what do they loudly and proudly say?

GLOSSARY

Gender identity: A person's sense of their own gender, which may or may not correspond to the sex they were assigned at birth.

Pronouns: Words we use to refer to someone's gender in conversation, for example "he/his" or "she/her." Some people use gender-neutral pronouns such as "they/their" or "zie/zir."

Trans: An umbrella term used to describe someone whose gender is not the same as, or does not align with, the sex they were assigned at birth.

Transition: The steps a trans person may take to live in the gender they identify as.

by the same author

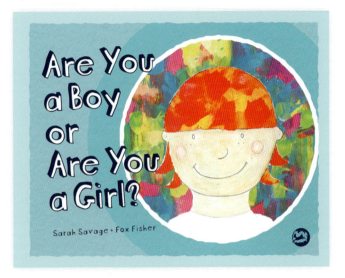

Tiny prefers not to tell other children whether they are a boy or girl. Tiny also loves to play fancy dress, sometimes as a fairy and sometimes as a knight in shining armour. Tiny's family don't seem to mind but when they start a new school some of their new classmates struggle to understand.

ISBN 978 1 78592 267 1 | eISBN 978 1 78450 556 1

of related interest

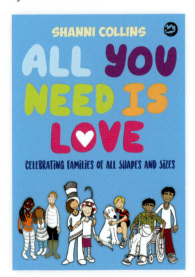

ISBN 978 1 78592 251 0
eISBN 978 1 78450 534 9

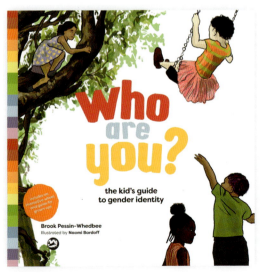

ISBN 978 1 78592 728 7
eISBN 978 1 78450 580 6

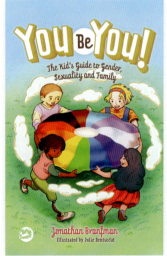

ISBN 978 1 78775 010 4
eISBN 978 1 78775 011 1